ROSEMARY WELLS

TIMOTHY GOES TO SCHOOL

SCHOLASTIC INC.

New York Toronto London Auckland Sydney
Mexico City New Delhi Hong Kong

ISBN 0-439-22707-0

12 11 10 9 8 7   4 5 6/0

Printed in the U.S.A.   40

First Scholastic printing, September 2000

The art for this book was prepared in the usual way: with watercolor, pen and ink, gouache, pastel, and rubber stamps.

For Mimi Kayden

TIMOTHY'S mother made him a brand-new sunsuit for the first day of school.
"Hooray!" said Timothy.

Timothy went to school in his new sunsuit
with his new book and his new pencil.

"Good morning!" said Timothy.
"Good morning!" said Mrs. Jenkins.

"Timothy," said Mrs. Jenkins, "this is Claude. Claude, this is Timothy. I'm sure you'll be the best of friends."

A B C D E F G H

"Hello!" said Timothy.
"Nobody wears a sunsuit on the first day of school," said Claude.

During playtime Timothy hoped and
hoped that Claude would fall into a puddle.

But he didn't.

When Timothy came home, his mother asked,
"How was school today?"

"Nobody wears a sunsuit on the first day of school," said Timothy.

"I will make you a beautiful new jacket," said Timothy's mother.

Timothy wore his new jacket the next day.

"Hello!" said Timothy to Claude.
"You're not supposed to wear party clothes
on the second day of school," said Claude.

All day Timothy wanted and wanted Claude
to make a mistake.

But he didn't.

When Timothy went home, his mother asked,
"How did it go?"

"You're not supposed to wear party clothes
on the second day of school," said Timothy.

"Don't worry," said Timothy's mother.
"Tomorrow you just wear something in-between
like everyone else."

The next day Timothy went to school in his favorite shirt.

"Look!" said Timothy. "You are wearing the same shirt I am!"

"No," said Claude, "*you* are wearing the same shirt that *I* am."

During lunch Timothy wished and wished
that Claude would have to eat all alone.

But he didn't.

After school Timothy's mother could not find
Timothy. "Where are you?" she called.
"I'm never going back to school," said Timothy.
"Why not?" called his mother.

"Because Claude is the smartest and the best at everything and he has all the friends," said Timothy.

"You'll feel better in your new football shirt," said Timothy's mother.

Timothy did not feel better in his new football shirt.

That morning Claude played the saxophone.
"I can't stand it anymore," said a voice next to
Timothy.

It was Violet.
"You can't stand what?" Timothy asked Violet.

"Grace!" said Violet. "She sings. She dances. She counts up to a thousand and she sits next to me!"

During playtime Timothy and Violet
stayed together.

Violet said, "I can't believe you've been here all along!"

"Will you come home and have cookies with me after school?" Timothy asked.

On the way home Timothy and Violet laughed
so much about Claude and Grace that they both
got the hiccups.